GOD BLESS AMERICA

The Story of an Immigrant Named Irving Berlin

WRITTEN BY **Adah Nuchi**   ILLUSTRATED BY **Rob Polivka**

Disney • HYPERION

Los Angeles   New York

For my parents, who immigrated
–A.N.

For the immigrants whose songs we were not
blessed to hear –R.P.

The Bowery was bustling!

Vendors barked and shoppers shouted,
dogs growled and babies howled,
beggars, policemen,
pushcarts, trolleys,
and Chinese, Italian, Irish, and Jewish immigrants
all swarmed the busy street.

And right in the middle,
Izzy Baline had
a *thump-two-three,
ting-a-ling, whee* song.

Plink! A coin landed at Izzy's feet.
Plunk! Another one.

Izzy was peddling newspapers, and a song with the evening news could mean an extra coin tossed his way.

Izzy Baline always had a song.

In Russia,
where Izzy was born, it was to the
zim-a-lay-quiver,
weep, call, waver
prayers his forefathers had chanted
for thousands of years.

But Izzy's family was chased out of Russia for being Jews. They joined the throngs of immigrants escaping for a better, safer life, and boarded a ship to . . .

On New York's Lower East Side,
where Izzy and his family crowded eight people
into one tiny apartment,
where the streets were crowded too,
no one had time for a song.

Only the factories hummed
from dawn till dusk,
as everyone scrambled
to make ends meet.

Still, Izzy's mother murmured,
"God bless America,"
and they all agreed.
America had taken them in.

But when Izzy's father died
and they had even less,
it was time to see what else America could bring.
Out on his own, Izzy
zipped up the Bowery. He didn't stop singing
until he hit a street
bursting with music publishers.

In Tin Pan Alley,
everything rang!
Music clanged out of windows
and tinkled through the air,
black and white notes danced off the presses,
and Izzy cranked out tune after tune after tune.

He was going to be a songwriter.

Izzy couldn't read or write music, but he composed the words. And he hummed the melodies for someone else to jot down. By the time he was twenty-six, he had written two hundred songs. He also gave himself a new name: Irving Berlin.

But at night, while soldiers tossed and turned and creaked and snored,
Irving lay wide-awake, composing.
He had a *toot-a-root soar,*
whisper, rise, blare song.

Soon, instead of selling newspapers, he was making headlines.
America had fallen in love with Irving Berlin.

Irving Berlin had fallen in love
with America, too.
He took the oath to become a citizen,
and with his country at war,
Irving joined the
cloppity-clop-thwack
march, tramp, pow
rhythms of the United States Army.

Irving was a songwriter, not a soldier.
There was a better way for him to
help his country: a musical for the army.
Irving wrote all the songs.

One was from the words his mother used to say.
A song called "God Bless America."
But the song wasn't right for his show, and
Irving tucked it away.

Two decades later, America marched toward an even bigger war.

People needed their spirits warmed, their fears quelled,

and something grand to cheer for.

Irving Berlin needed a song.

Not a *tap-tappity-tap* song
like the ones he wrote for Broadway,

not a *scat-a-tat-tat* song like the ones he wrote for Hollywood,

and not the songs that swung high and moaned low like the ones he wrote for the people he loved.

Irving Berlin needed
a *boom-rah-rah* song.
A big brass belter.
A loud heart melter.
A song for America.

He went to his box of unused songs, searching for inspiration. There he found a song with *boom-rah-rah*, and this time it was right. Irving tweaked the lyrics and tinkered with the tune.

On Armistice Day, 1938, when "God Bless America" filled the radio,

when the American people hummed it at home

and roared it
in stadiums,

and listened to it over and over and over,
everyone had a *boom-rah-rah* song.

A song for America to sing.

And while some people didn't like that
the voice of America belonged to an immigrant
and a Jew, most people felt that a refugee
was just the right person to celebrate
the hope America held.

Three presidents of the United States agreed
and gave Irving medals for his devotion to his country.

Irving Berlin had
a *boom-rah-rah* song
because America had given him
a reason to sing.

America had a song too,
because America had
Irving Berlin.

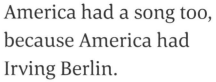

Irving Berlin was born Israel (Izzy) Baline—originally spelled Beilin—in Russia on May 11, 1888. It was a period of great turmoil in Russia, and between the years 1881 and 1921, pogroms—widespread violence and raids on Jewish villages—forced approximately two million Jews to flee their homes. Izzy's earliest memory was watching his home burn down in a pogrom. His family was lucky to escape. They were also lucky that America was willing to take them in. On September 13, 1893, they landed in New York City.

Life in America wasn't easy for the Baline family. In Russia, Izzy's father, Moses, had been a cantor—or singer—in their synagogue. Now he worked three jobs and still struggled to make ends meet. The rest of the Balines all had to help. Izzy's siblings went to work in factories. Izzy was too young to work in a factory, so he sold newspapers. But Izzy didn't contribute as much as his siblings did, and he worried about becoming a burden, especially after his father died. He decided to see if he'd have any luck out on his own, and when he was thirteen years old, he ran away from home.

Izzy had a lot of jobs. Eventually he found work as a singing waiter. He mostly sang other people's songs, but sometimes he made up little ditties of his own. So when Izzy's boss wanted one of his waiters to write a song, Izzy teamed up with the restaurant's pianist to compose "Marie from Sunny Italy." Izzy ran with his song straight to Tin Pan Alley, a street in Manhattan where all of the music publishers were clustered together, to see if he could get it published. He could, and he did! But there was a typo on the page. It said the song had been written by I. Berlin. Soon after that, Izzy adopted the name Irving Berlin.

Now that Irving was a published songwriter, he got a job writing songs in Tin Pan Alley. He couldn't read or write music, so he would write the lyrics and someone else would come up with the tune, or he would hum what he had in mind for someone to write down. Eventually he learned to pick out some of his melodies on the piano. Irving wrote a lot of songs. In fact, he wrote so many that he was quickly becoming one of America's most popular songwriters.

Then America went to war. Irving wrote many songs about the war. He even wrote a song encouraging Americans to enlist in the army. But Irving himself couldn't enlist. He had never officially become an American citizen. In 1918, at the age of twenty-nine, he took an oath and became a citizen. A few months later, he was drafted into the army.

Irving loved America, but he didn't love being a soldier. That's because soldiers had to wake up early in the morning. He hated waking up so much that he wrote a song called "Oh! How I Hate to Get Up in the Morning." Everyone loved the song. (They also hated getting up in the morning.) That gave Irving an idea. He asked his general if he could make a show to promote the army. He would write songs about army life, and use soldiers to perform them. The general thought it was a great idea. He even gave Irving permission to work on the show whenever he wanted. Now Irving didn't have to get up in the morning!

But Irving did have to write a show. He gathered more than three hundred troops to serve as his cast and crew. Then he wrote his songs. One of the songs he wrote was called "God Bless America." It was a phrase Irving's mother used to say, even when things were tough. After all, America had given them a new home. But the song Irving wrote didn't quite fit the whole show. He put the song away.

Twenty years later, the world was facing another war. By now Irving was a huge star, writing for Hollywood and Broadway. He wanted to write a peace song for his country, but he couldn't come up with the right words. Then he remembered "God Bless America." Perhaps this time it would be right.

On Armistice Day in 1938, the singer Kate Smith debuted the song on the radio. People liked the song so much that they wanted to replace the national anthem with it. But not everyone felt that way. Some people wanted to boycott the song because Irving was an immigrant and a Jew. But for every person who spoke out against the song, many more believed in it. Irving gave all the money he earned from "God Bless America" to the Girl Scouts and Boy Scouts of America.

Irving wasn't done giving back to America. He decided to return to the army and put on a show, just like the show he had put on before. Except this time Irving had a request. Blacks and whites didn't serve in the same units in the army, but Irving wanted both black and white actors to be in his show. His became the first integrated unit in uniform in World War II. Irving staged the show on Broadway. Then he took it on the road across America, and finally across the world. The show was even turned into a movie. Irving's show raised $10 million for the Army Emergency Relief Fund. Irving had done so much for America that President Truman gave him a Medal of Merit for a high standard of devotion to his country.

Irving Berlin died on September 22, 1989, at the age of 101. He wrote more than fifteen hundred songs in his lifetime. Many—including "White Christmas" and "God Bless America"—we still sing today. He was best known as a songwriter, but he was also an immigrant, a refugee, and most proudly, an American.

TIME LINE

1888: On May 11, Israel "Izzy" Beilin is born in Russia.

1893: Fleeing pogroms in Russia, Izzy, his parents, and five of his brothers and sisters settle in New York City's Lower East Side. They change the spelling of their name to Baline.

1901: Izzy's father, Moses, passes away. Shortly after, Izzy leaves home.

1907: Izzy's first song, "Marie from Sunny Italy," is published. A typo reading "Words by I. Berlin" gives Izzy his new name: Irving Berlin.

1911: Irving has his first big hit with "Alexander's Ragtime Band." The sheet music for the song sells a million copies in its first year of publication.

1912: Irving marries Dorothy Goetz, but she dies of typhoid fever only a few months later. Irving writes the song "When I Lost You" about her.

1914: The world goes to war on July 28. Two and a half years later, in 1917, the United States joins the fight.

1918: In February, Irving Berlin takes the oath and becomes a citizen of the United States of America. A few months later, he's drafted into the US Army and is sent to Camp Upton in New York.

1918: Irving writes "Oh! How I Hate to Get Up in the Morning" while serving in the army. The song's popularity among soldiers leads Irving to suggest creating a fundraising show for the army. *Yip! Yip! Yaphank* uses 300 soldiers as cast and crew. One of the songs Irving writes for the show is called "God Bless America." But he puts it aside to use another time.

1926: Irving marries again, this time to Ellin Mackay. He writes the song "Always" as a wedding gift to her.

1927: *The Jazz Singer*, the first full-length movie featuring synchronized music and talking, features Irving's "Blue Skies."

1930s: The rise of "talkies" (movies with synchronized sound) helps Irving find success in Hollywood. He writes the score for movies such as the Fred Astaire and Ginger Rogers hit *Top Hat,* which brings him his first Academy Award nomination with the song "Cheek to Cheek."

1938: With the world on the brink of another war, Irving wants to write a song for his country. He remembers "God Bless America," which he wrote 20 years earlier. He tweaks the lyrics and gives it to the singer Kate Smith. The song debuts on Armistice Day.

1940: Irving creates the God Bless America Fund, donating all of his royalties from the song to the Boy Scouts of America and Girl Scouts of America.

1941: The United States goes back to war.

1942: A few months after the United States enters WWII, Irving goes back to the army, this time as a volunteer. He's there to write another show: *This Is the Army.*

1942: The movie *Holiday Inn* is released, featuring the song "White Christmas," which would give Irving his only Academy Award for best song (though he is nominated an additional six times).

1943: A movie version of *This Is the Army* is made,

earning close to $10 million for the Army Emergency Relief Fund. The company embarks on a world tour.

1945: President Truman awards Irving the army's Medal of Merit for his patriotism.

1946: After the war, Irving returns to Broadway and Hollywood, writing the music for, among other musicals, *Annie Get Your Gun.*

1954: President Eisenhower gives Irving a Congressional Gold Medal for the song "God Bless America."

1966: Following "An Old-Fashioned Wedding," which he writes for a revival of *Annie Get Your Gun,* Irving retires from songwriting.

1977: President Ford presents Irving Berlin with the Presidential Medal of Freedom.

1988: Irving Berlin's 100th birthday is celebrated in a star-studded event at Carnegie Hall, and showcases many of his songs.

1989: On September 22, 1989, at the age of 101, Irving Berlin dies at home. He had written over 1500 songs throughout his life.

Ten Irving Berlin Songs You Might Be Familiar With:

Always

Anything You Can Do (I Can Do Better)

Blue Skies

Cheek to Cheek

Easter Parade

God Bless America

Puttin' On the Ritz

Steppin' Out with My Baby

There's No Business Like Show Business

White Christmas

To learn more about Irving Berlin and the music he wrote, visit these websites:

http://www.pbs.org/wnet/broadway/stars/irving-berlin/

https://www.biography.com/people/irving-berlin-9209473

http://parlorsongs.com/insearch/tinpanalley/tinpanalley.php

SELECTED SOURCES

Bergreen, Laurence. "Irving Berlin: This is the Army." *Prologue Magazine,* Summer 1996, Vol. 28, No. 2.

Furia, Philip. *Irving Berlin: A Life in Song.* New York: Schirmer Books, 1998.

Jablonski, Edward. *Irving Berlin: American Troubadour.* New York: Henry Holt, 1999.

Kaskowitz, Sheryl. *God Bless America: The Surprising History of an Iconic Song.* New York: Oxford University Press, 2013.

Shaw, John. *This Land That I Love: Irving Berlin, Woody Guthrie, and the Story of Two American Anthems.* New York: Public Affairs, 2013.

Woolf, S. J. "What Makes a Song: A Talk with Irving Berlin." *New York Times,* July 28, 1940, page 9.